Little Red Riding Hood

Harry Bornstein and Karen L. Saulnier
Illustrated by Bradley O. Pomeroy

FOREST HOUSE™
School & Library Edition

Kendall Green Publications
Gallaudet University Press
Washington, D.C.

TOLD IN SIGNED ENGLISH

Kendall Green Publications
An imprint of Gallaudet University Press
Washington, D.C. 20002

Printed in the United States of America
Library of Congress Cataloging-in-Publication Data
Bornstein, Harry.
Little Red Riding Hood / Harry Bornstein and Karen L. Saulnier ; illustrated by Bradley O. Pomeroy.
p. cm. — (Signed English series)
Summary: The well-known fairy tale about a little girl who meets a wolf posing as her grandmother, accompanied by diagrams showing how to form the Signed English signs for each word of the text.
ISBN 0-930323-63-7 : $13.95
1. Sign language — Juvenile literature. [1. Fairy tales. 2. Folklore — Germany. 3. Sign language.] I. Saulnier, Karen Luczak. II. Pomeroy, Bradley O., ill. III. Title. IV. Series.
PZ8.B64378Li 1990
398.21 — dc20
[E]
90-3477
CIP
AC

PREFACE

Signed English is a communication system that allows its users to simultaneously say and sign the patterns of spoken English. Its manual component is based on American Sign Language, but includes invented signs and grammatical sign "markers." When properly implemented, Signed English provides an English-language environment in which hearing-impaired and other language-delayed children can learn the vocabulary and structure of English. In Signed English, each sign corresponds to one English word. Words that cannot be represented by signs can be fingerspelled using the American Manual Alphabet.

Signed English was designed to be used with speech. Hearing-impaired children learn English through a combination of hearing spoken words, speechreading, and seeing manual signs.

Little Red Riding Hood told in Signed English makes a well-known folktale accessible to hearing-impaired children in a new and inviting way. Read the story aloud to your child. Learn the signs so that you can read and sign the story at the same time. This will help your child to associate specific signs with specific English words and lip movements. Encourage your child to repeat the signs and words and to retell the story.

Many other stories and books are available in the Signed English Series. For more information, contact **Gallaudet University Press.**

AMERICAN MANUAL ALPHABET

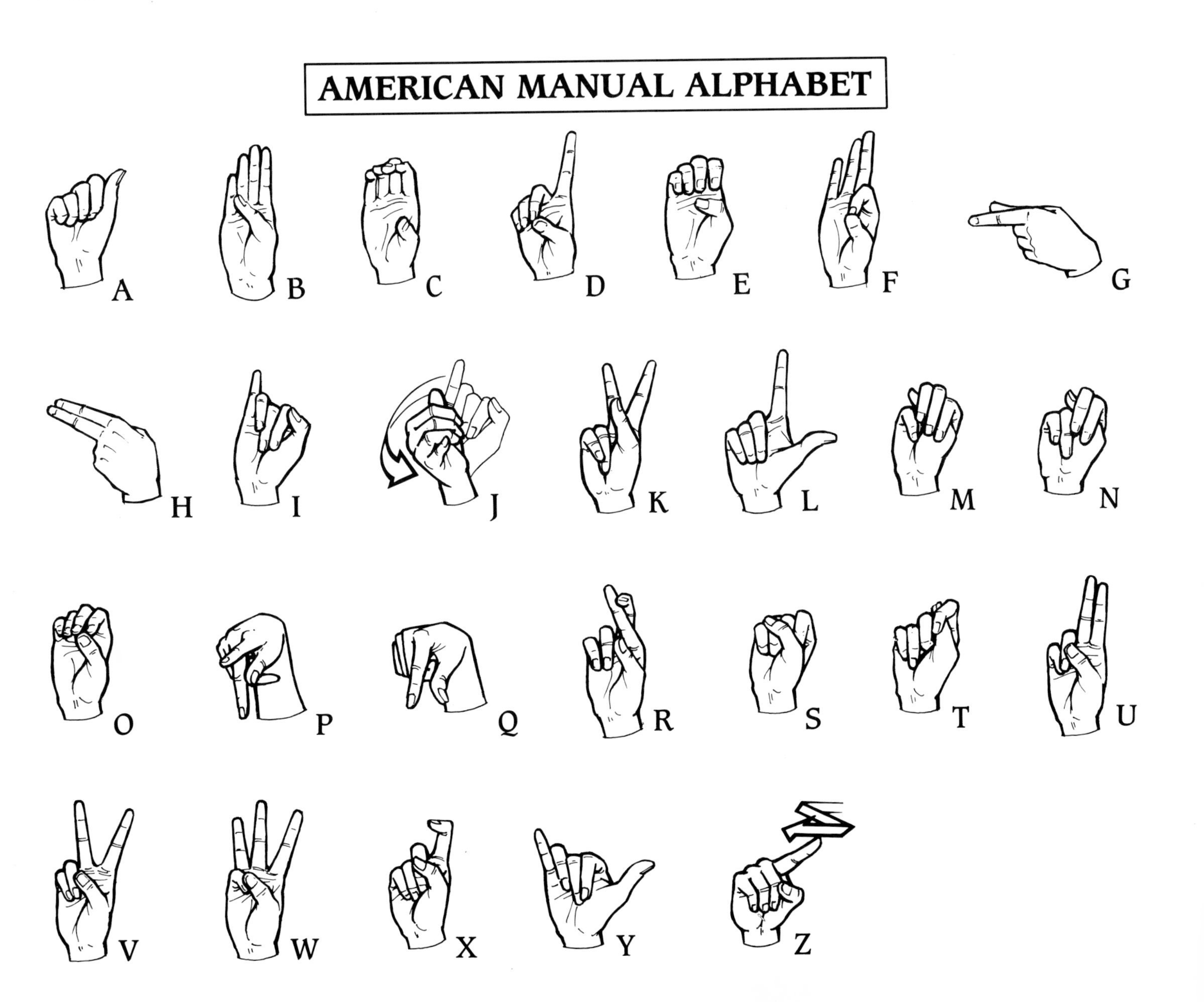

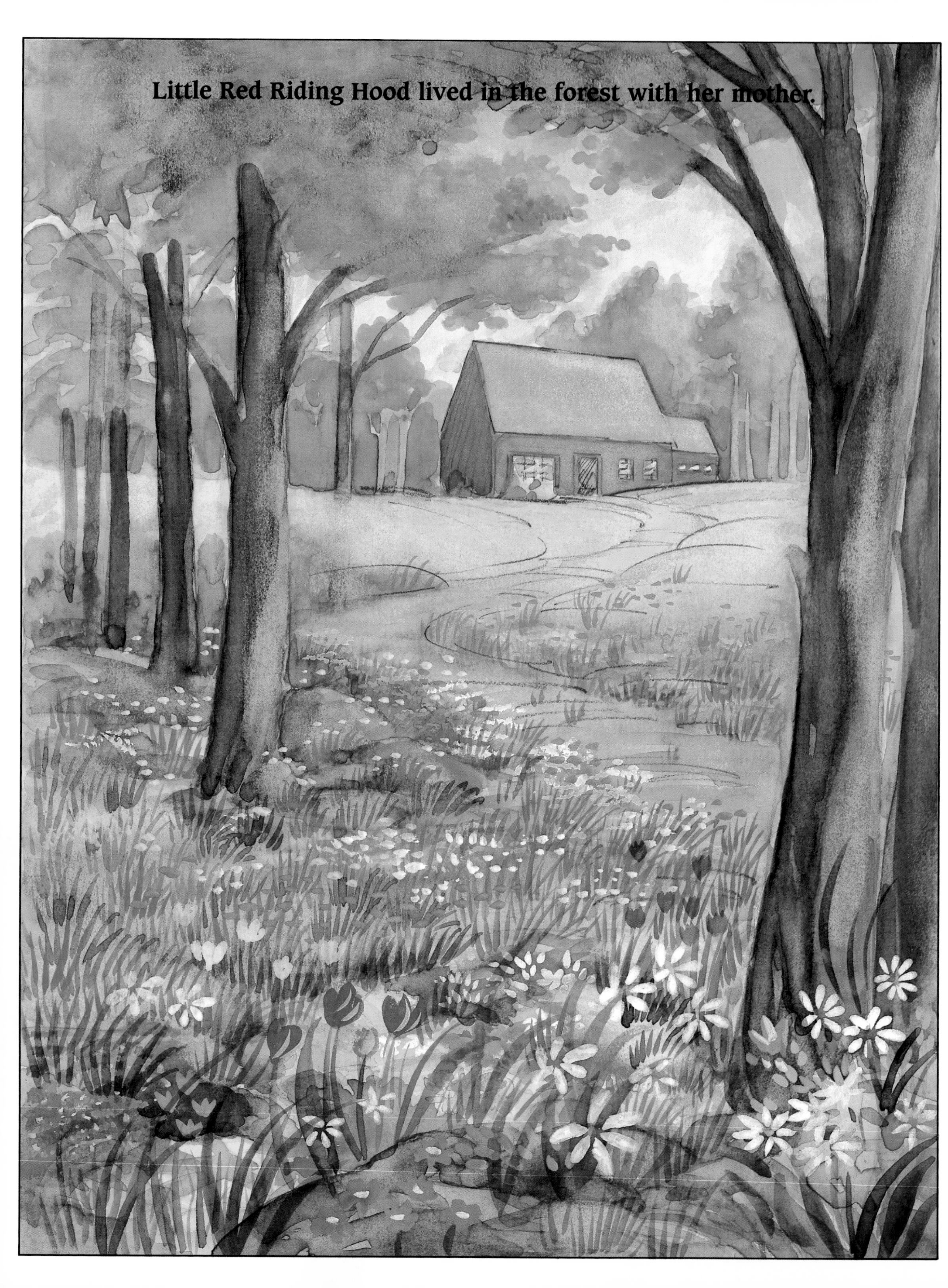
Little Red Riding Hood lived in the forest with her mother.

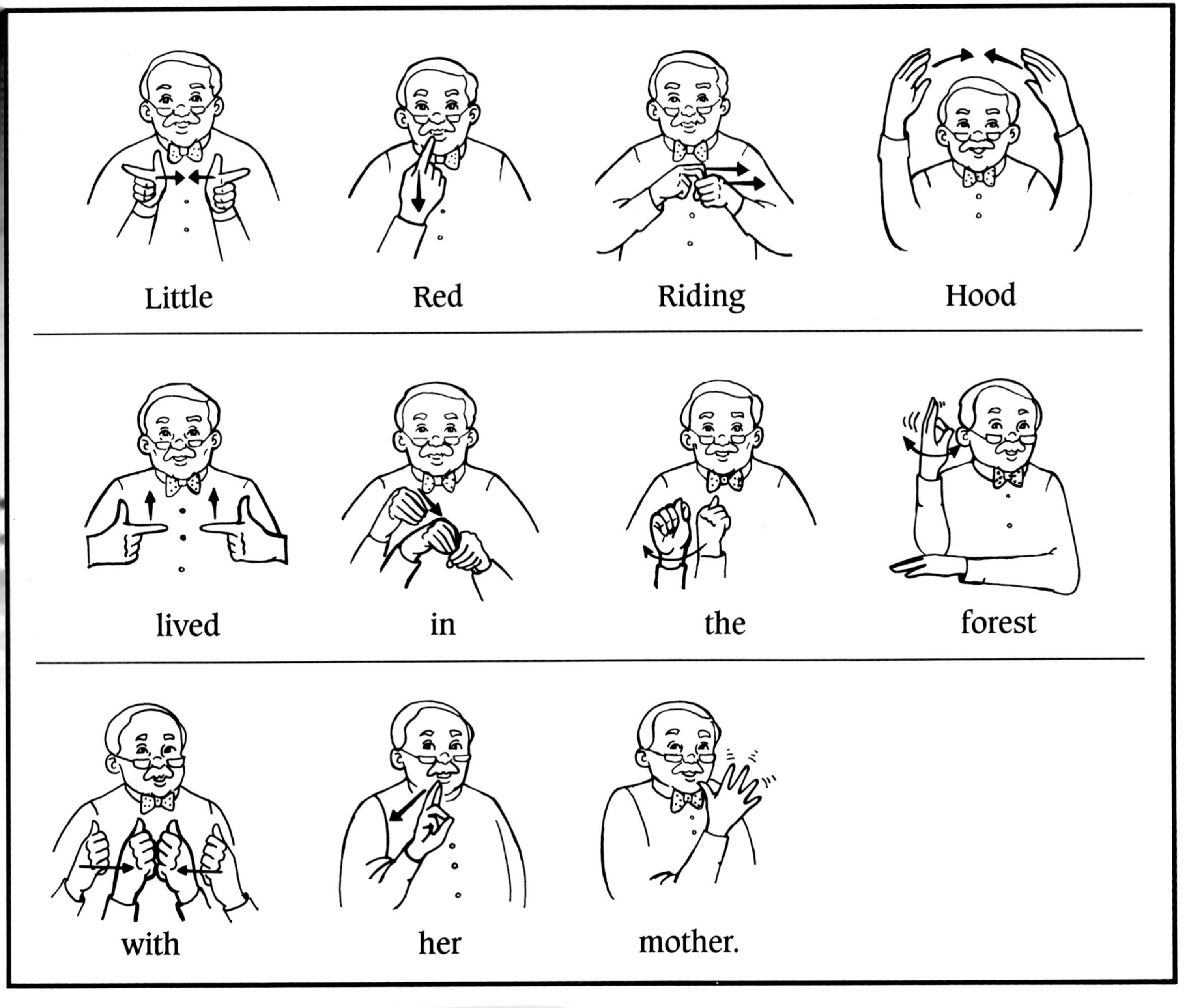
Little
Red
Riding
Hood
lived
in
the
forest
with
her
mother.

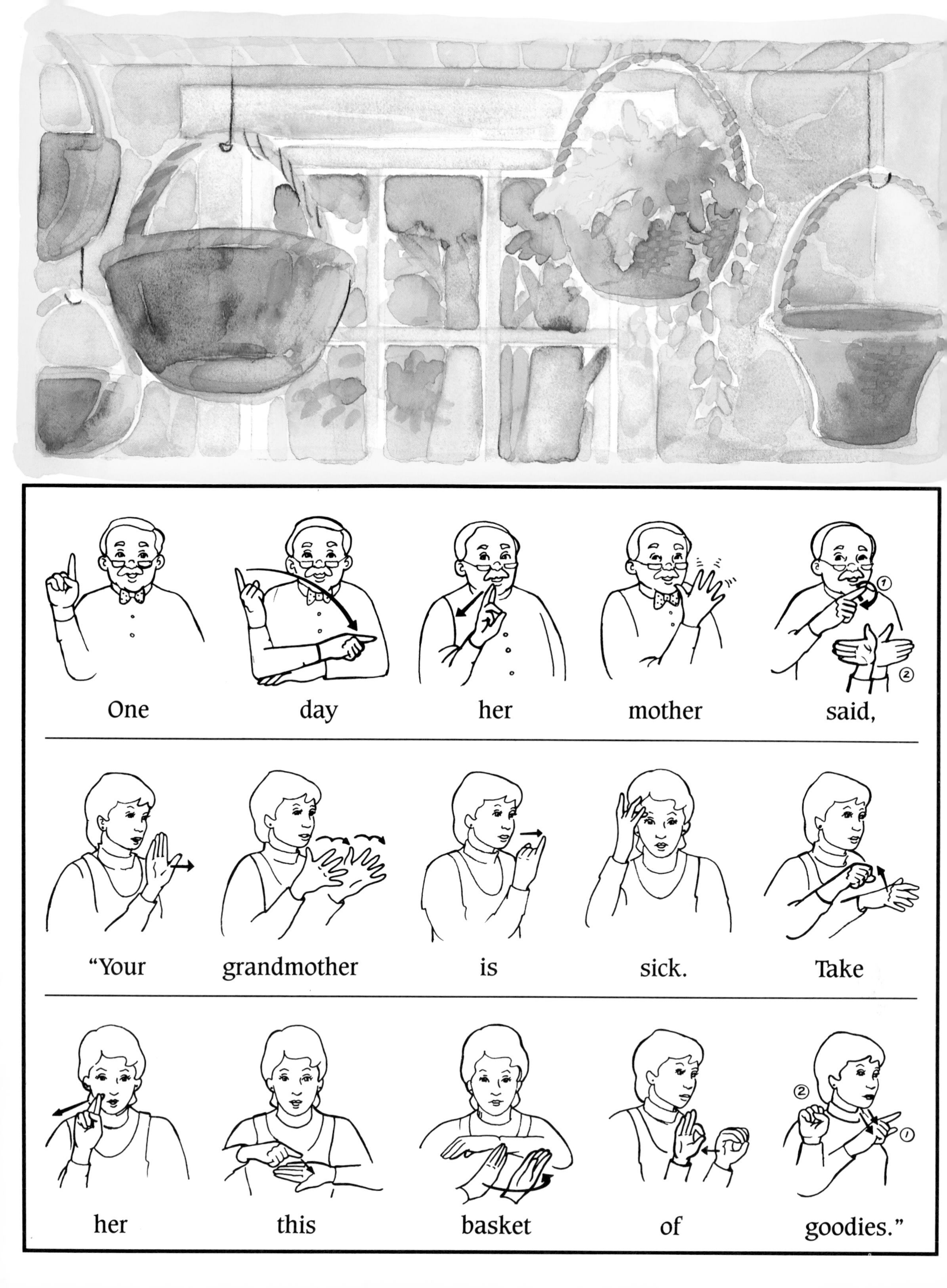

One
day
her
mother
said,
“Your
grandmother
is
sick.
Take
her
this
basket
of
goodies.”

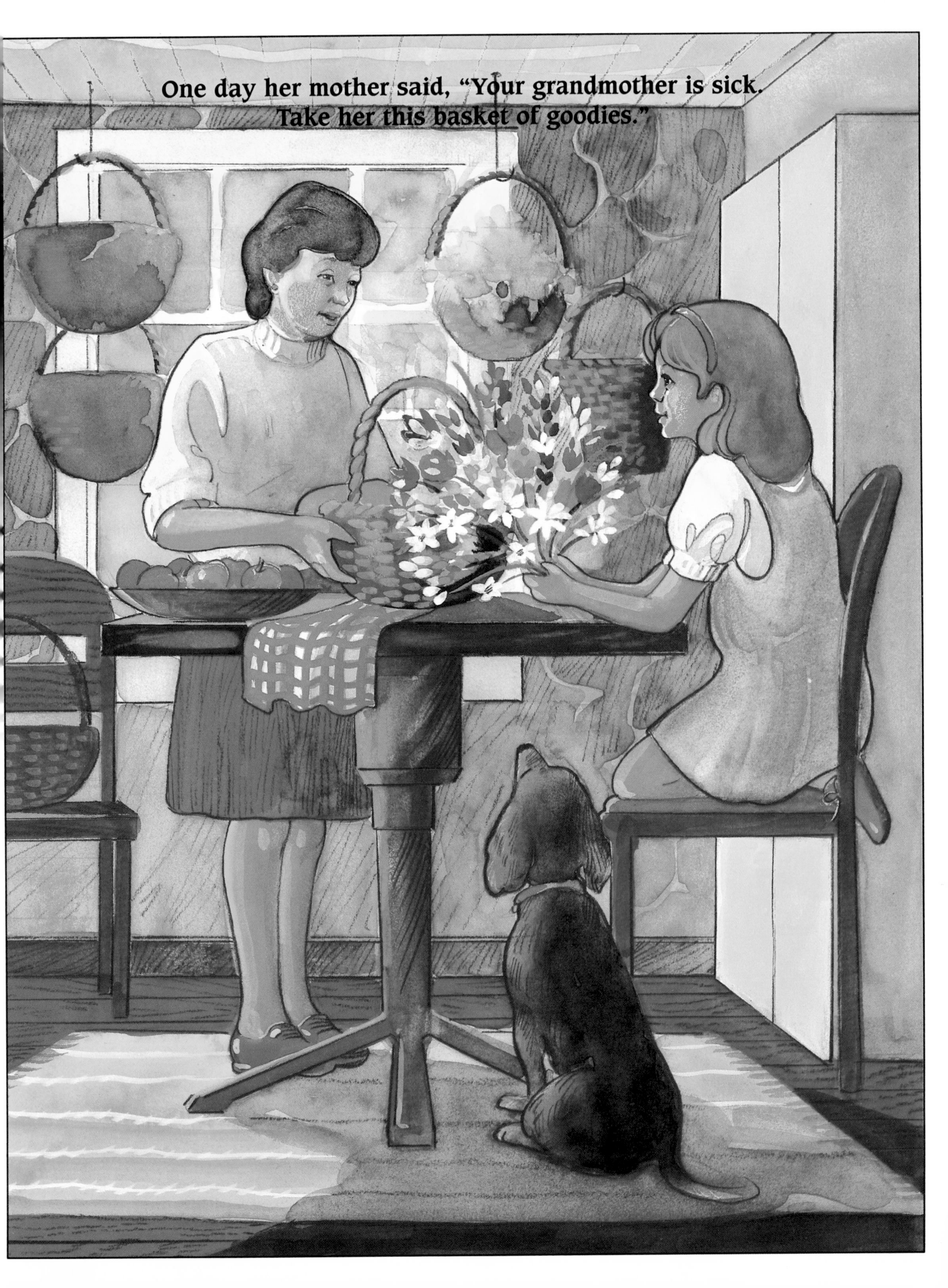

One day her mother said, "Your grandmother is sick.
Take her this basket of goodies."

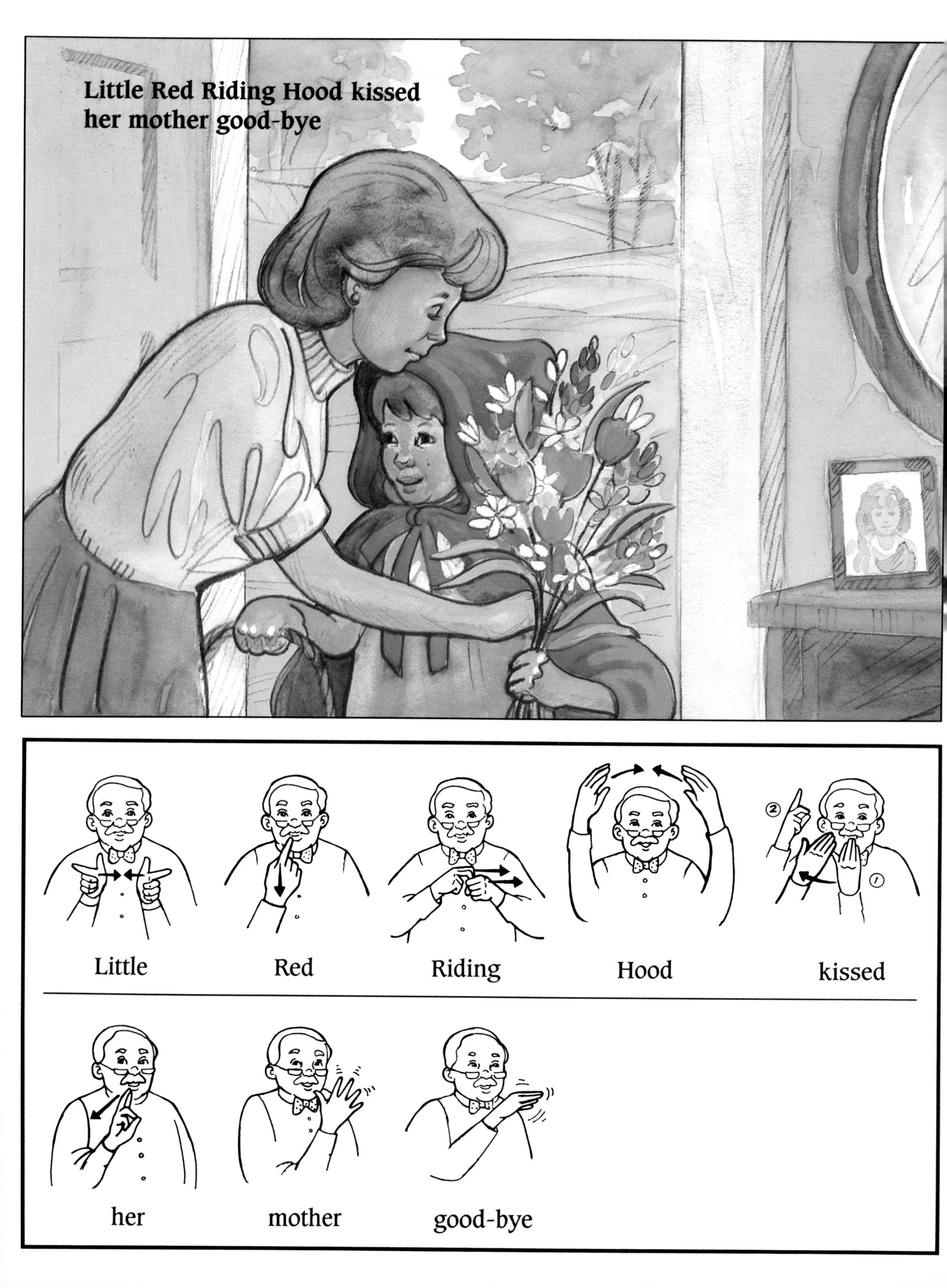
Little Red Riding Hood kissed
her mother good-bye
Little
Red
Riding
Hood
kissed
her
mother
good-bye

and
walked
happily
through
the
woods
to
Grandmother's
house.

and walked happily through the woods
to Grandmother's house.

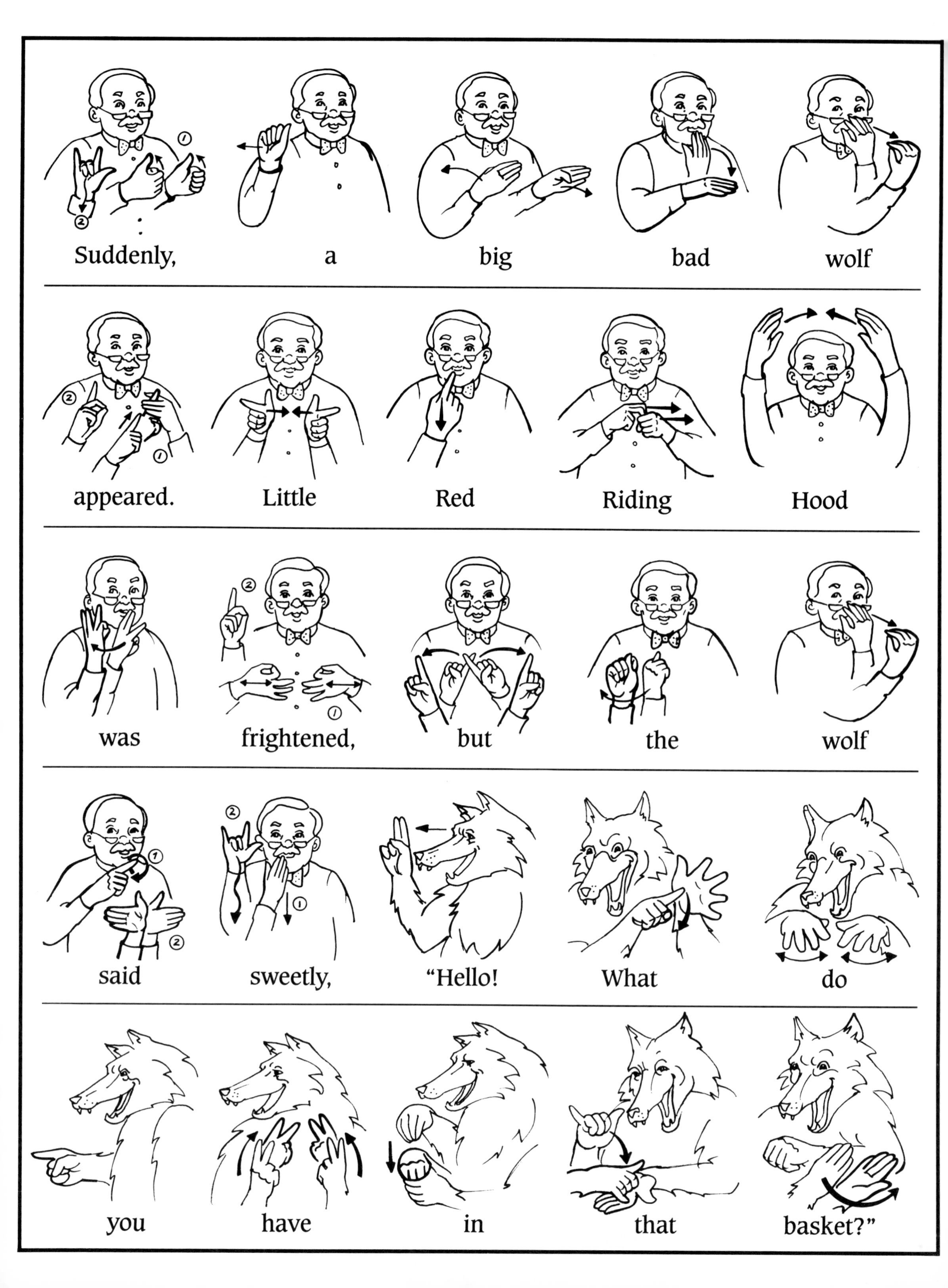

Suddenly,
a
big
bad
wolf
appeared.
Little
Red
Riding
Hood
was
frightened,
but
the
wolf
said
sweetly,
"Hello!
What
do
you
have
in
that
basket?"

Suddenly, a big bad wolf appeared.
Little Red Riding Hood was frightened,
but the wolf said sweetly, "Hello!
What do you have in that basket?"

"I'm taking some goodies to my grandmother," she replied.

"I'm
taking
some
goodies
to
my
grandmother,"
she
replied.

"Oh? And where does your grandmother live?" asked the wolf.

"Oh?

And

where

does

your

grandmother

live?"

asked

the

wolf.

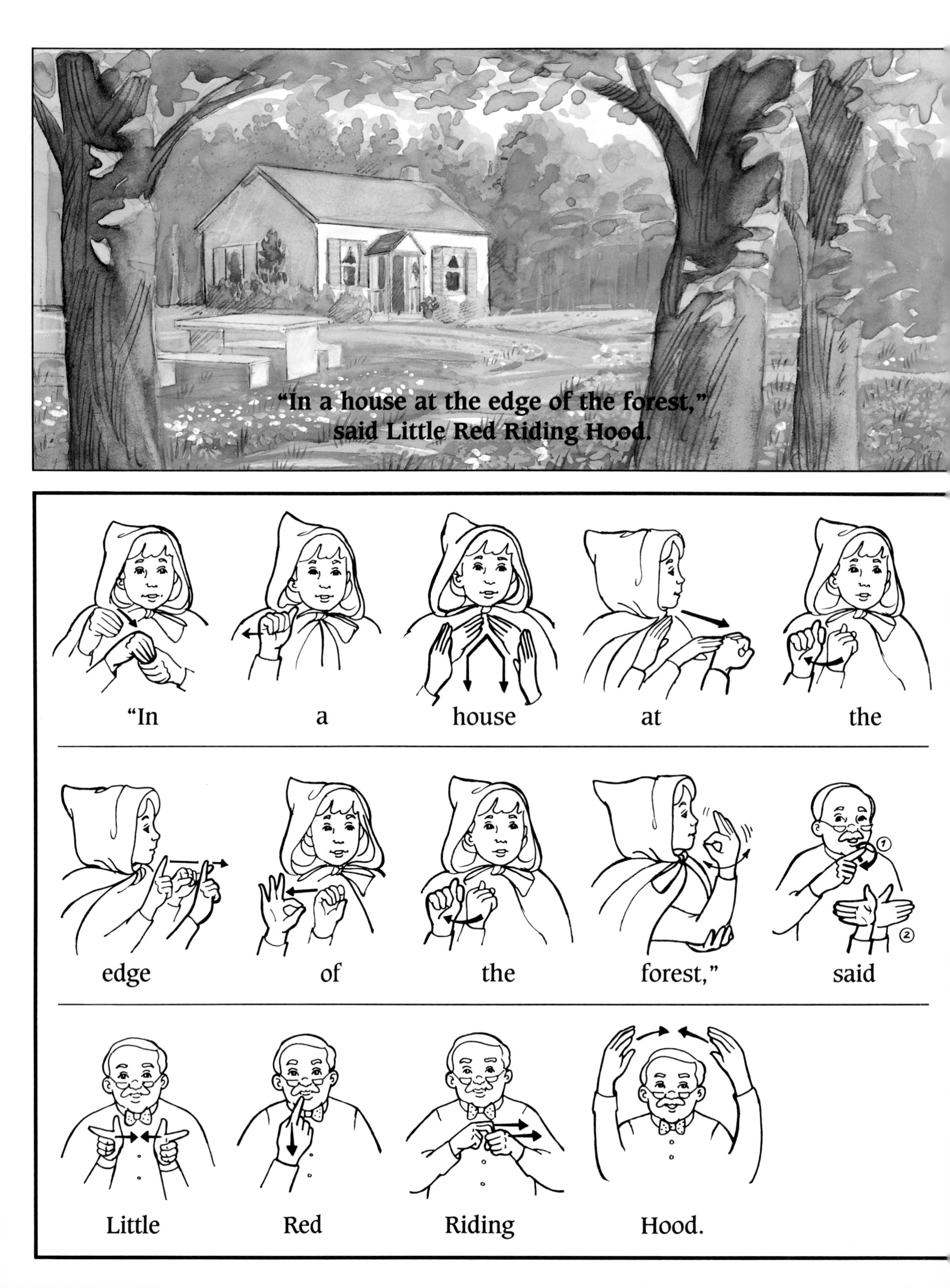
"In a house at the edge of the forest,"
said Little Red Riding Hood.
"In
a
house
at
the
edge
of
the
forest,"
said
Little
Red
Riding
Hood.

The
wolf
left
and
ran
quickly
to
Grandmother's
house.
The wolf left and ran quickly
to Grandmother's house.

He knocked on the door.

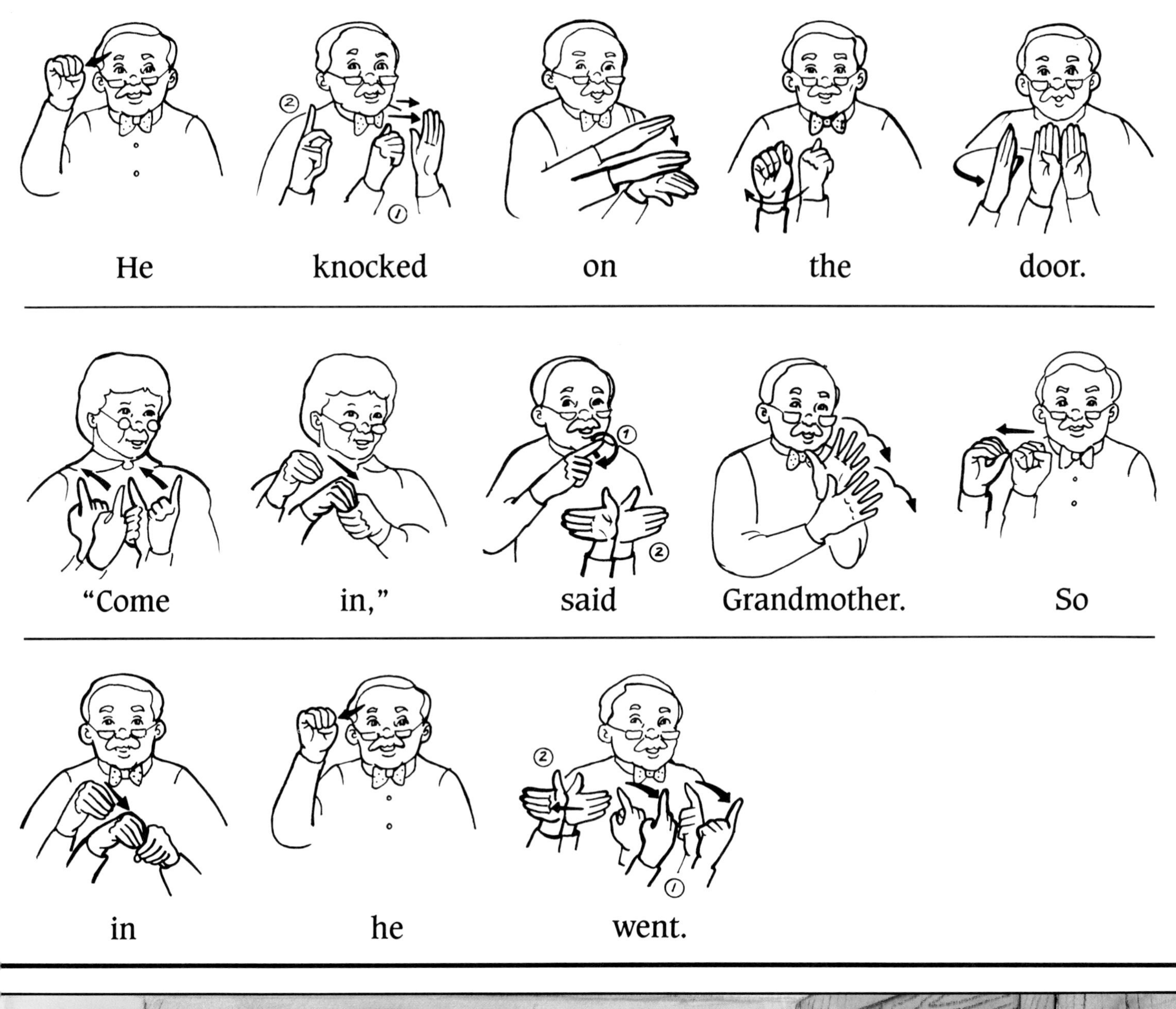
He
knocked
on
the
door.
“Come
in,”
said
Grandmother.
So
in
he
went.

“Come in,” sai
So in he went.

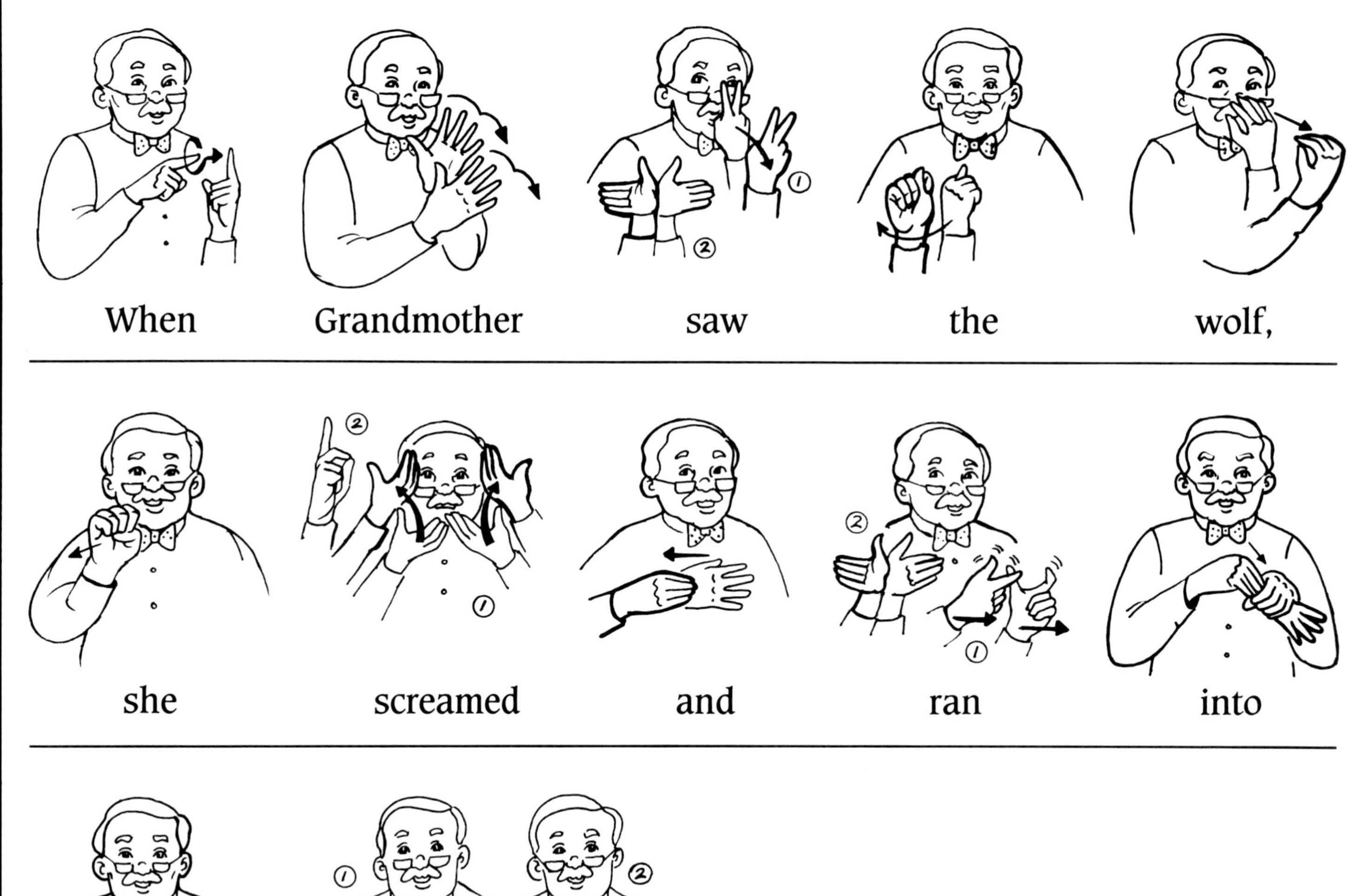
When Grandmother saw the wolf,
she screamed and ran into
the closet.

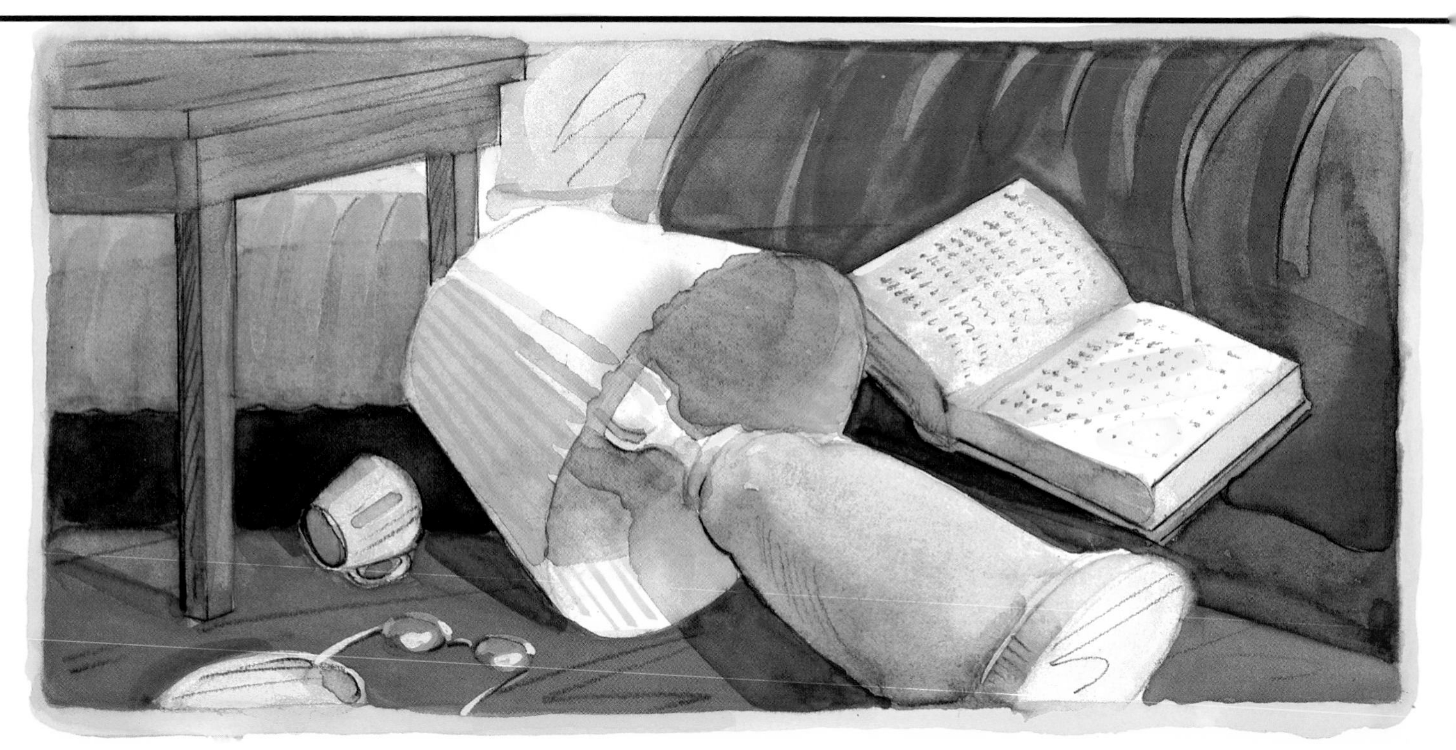

When Grandmother saw the wolf, she screamed and ran into the closet.

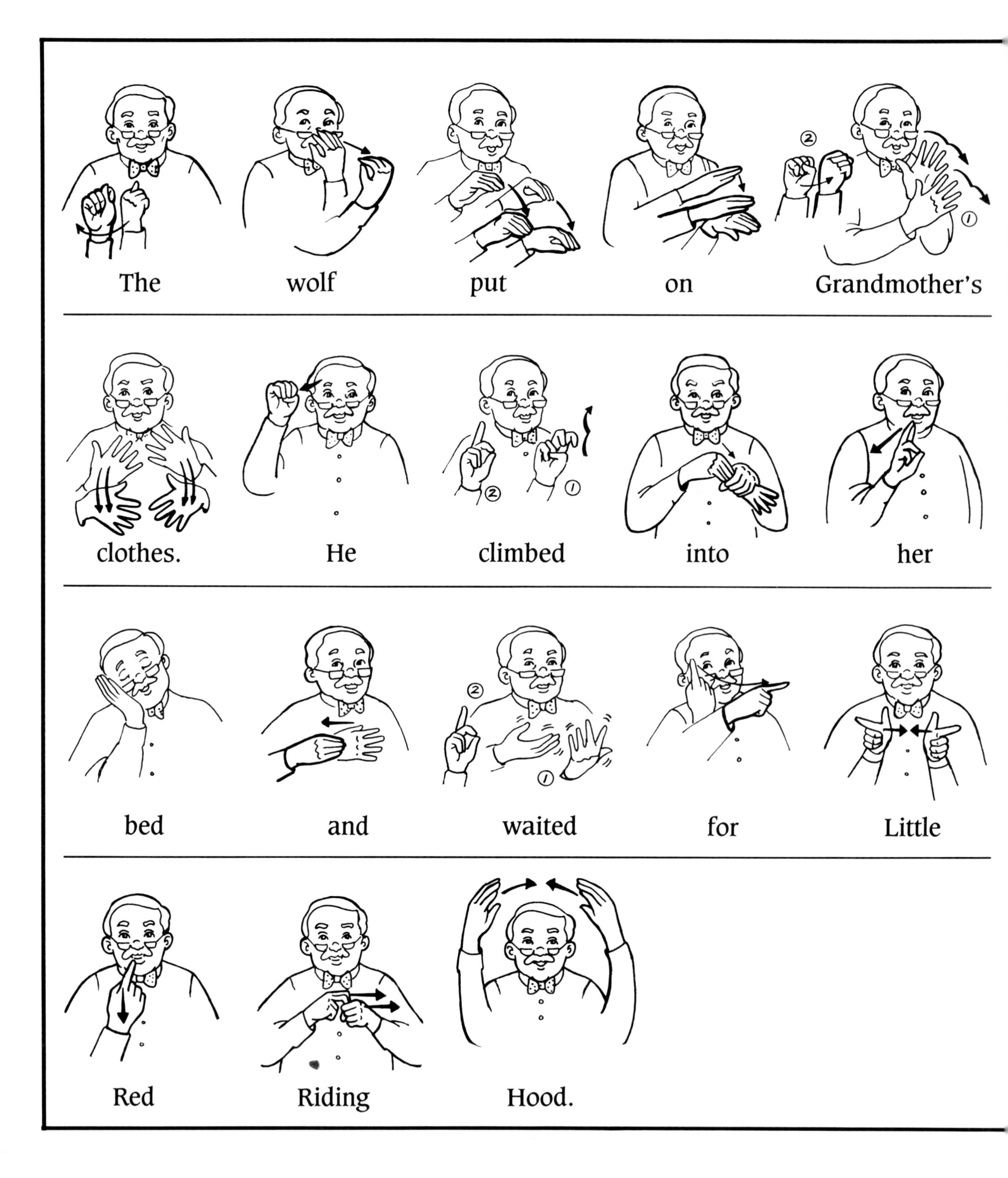

The
wolf
put
on
Grandmother's
clothes.
He
climbed
into
her
bed
and
waited
for
Little
Red
Riding
Hood.

The wolf put on Grandmother's clothes.
He climbed into her bed and waited
for Little Red Riding Hood.

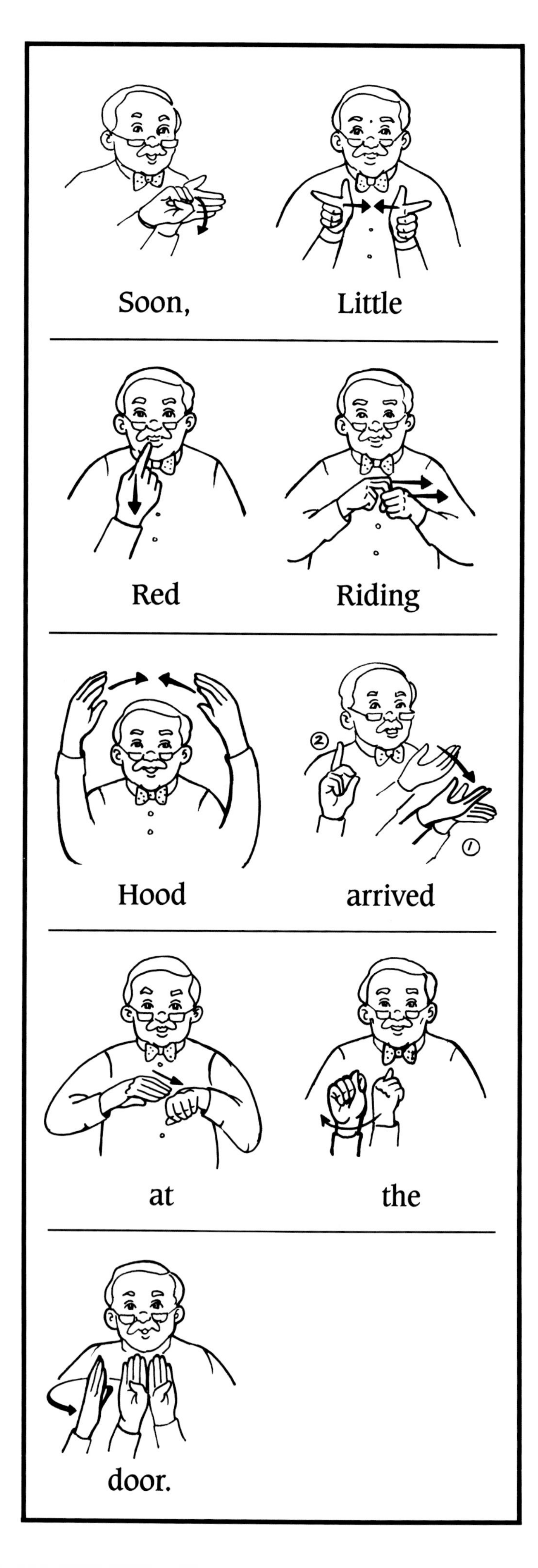
Soon,
Little
Red
Riding
Hood
arrived
at
the
door.

Soon, Little Red Riding Hood arriv

door.

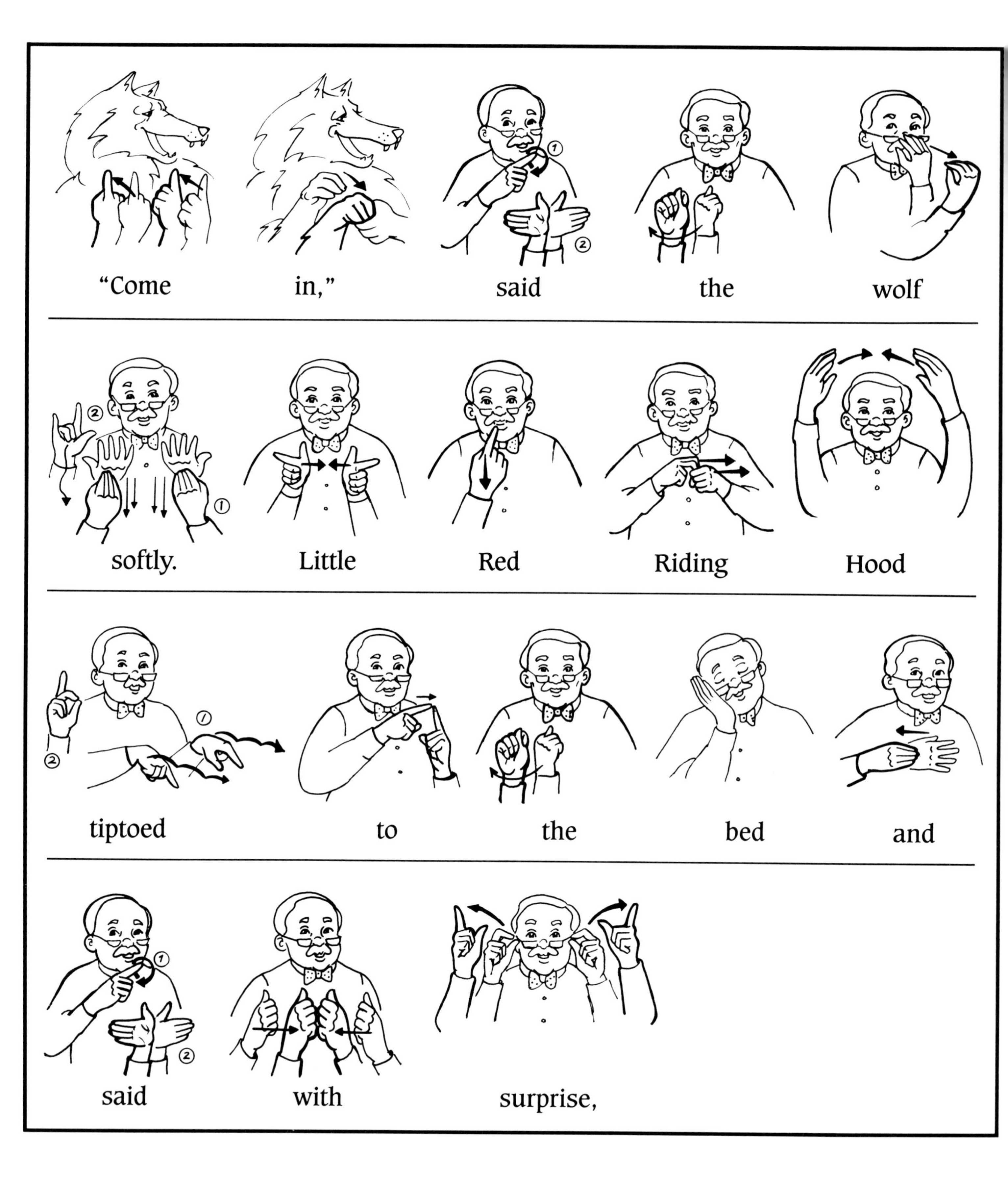
"Come
in,"
said
the
wolf
softly.
Little
Red
Riding
Hood
tiptoed
to
the
bed
and
said
with
surprise,

"Come in," said the wolf softly.
Little Red Riding Hood tiptoed
to the bed and said with surprise,

“Oh,
Grandmother,
what
big
eyes
you
have!”
“The
better
to

"Oh, Grandmother, what big eyes you have!"
"The better to see you with, my dear," answered the wolf.
see
you
with,
my
dear,"
answered
the
wolf.

"Oh, Grandmother, what big ears you have!"
"Oh,
Grandmother,
what
big
ears
you
have!"

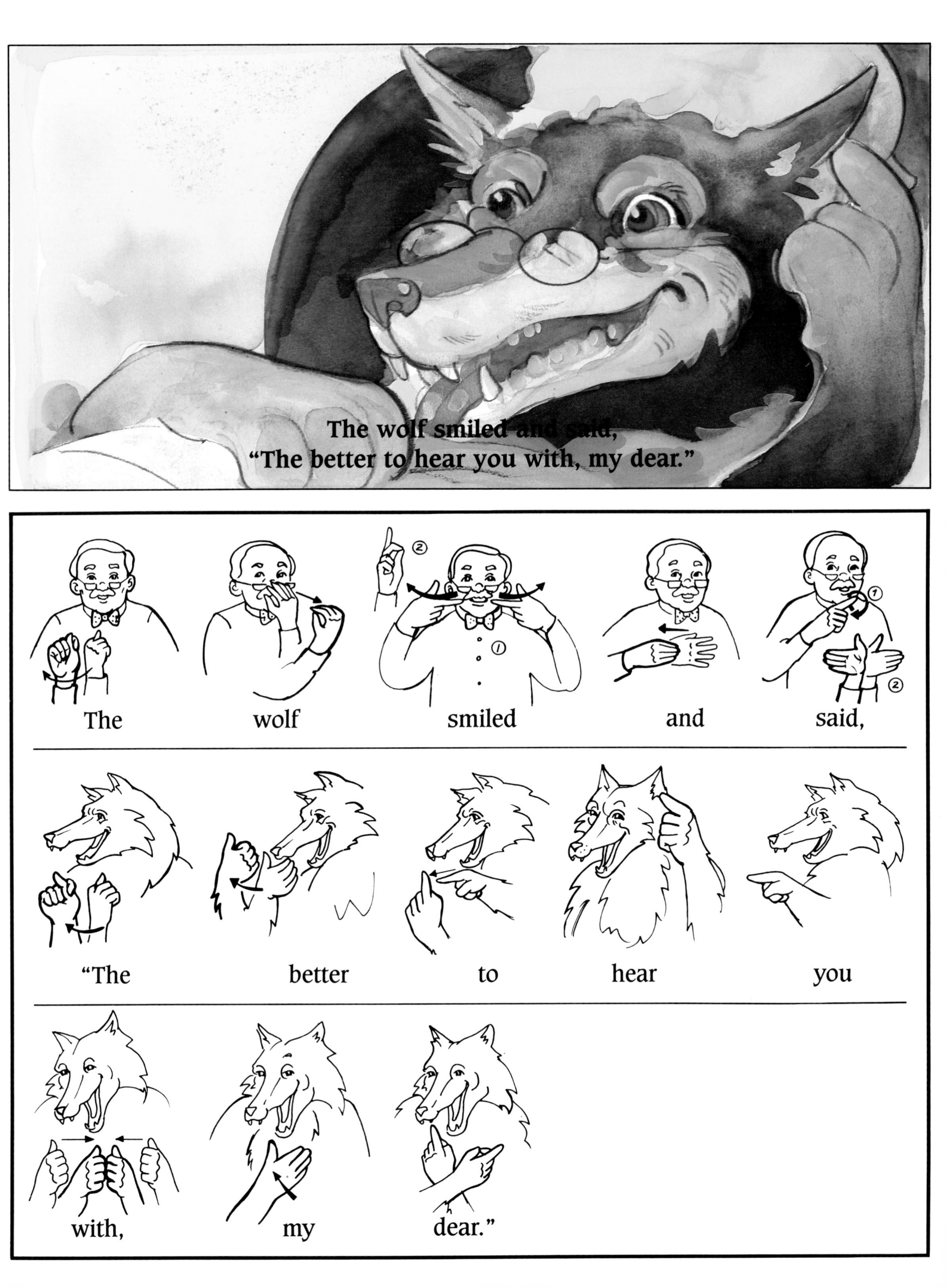
The wolf smiled and said,
"The better to hear you with, my dear."
The
wolf
smiled
and
said,
"The
better
to
hear
you
with,
my
dear."

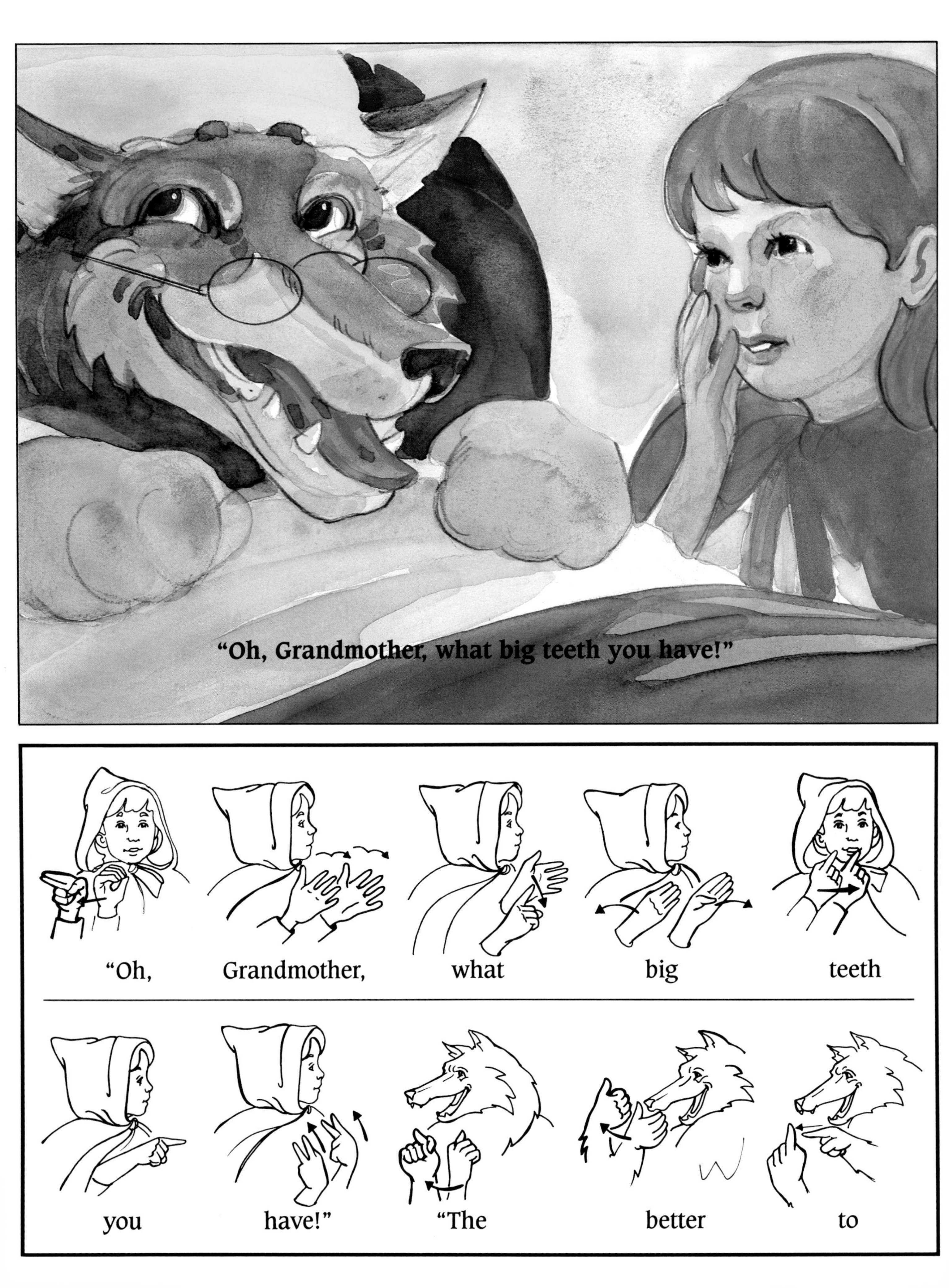
"Oh, Grandmother, what big teeth you have!"
"Oh,
Grandmother,
what
big
teeth
you
have!"
"The
better
to

"The better to eat you with my dear!" cried the wolf.

eat you with my dear!"

cried the wolf.

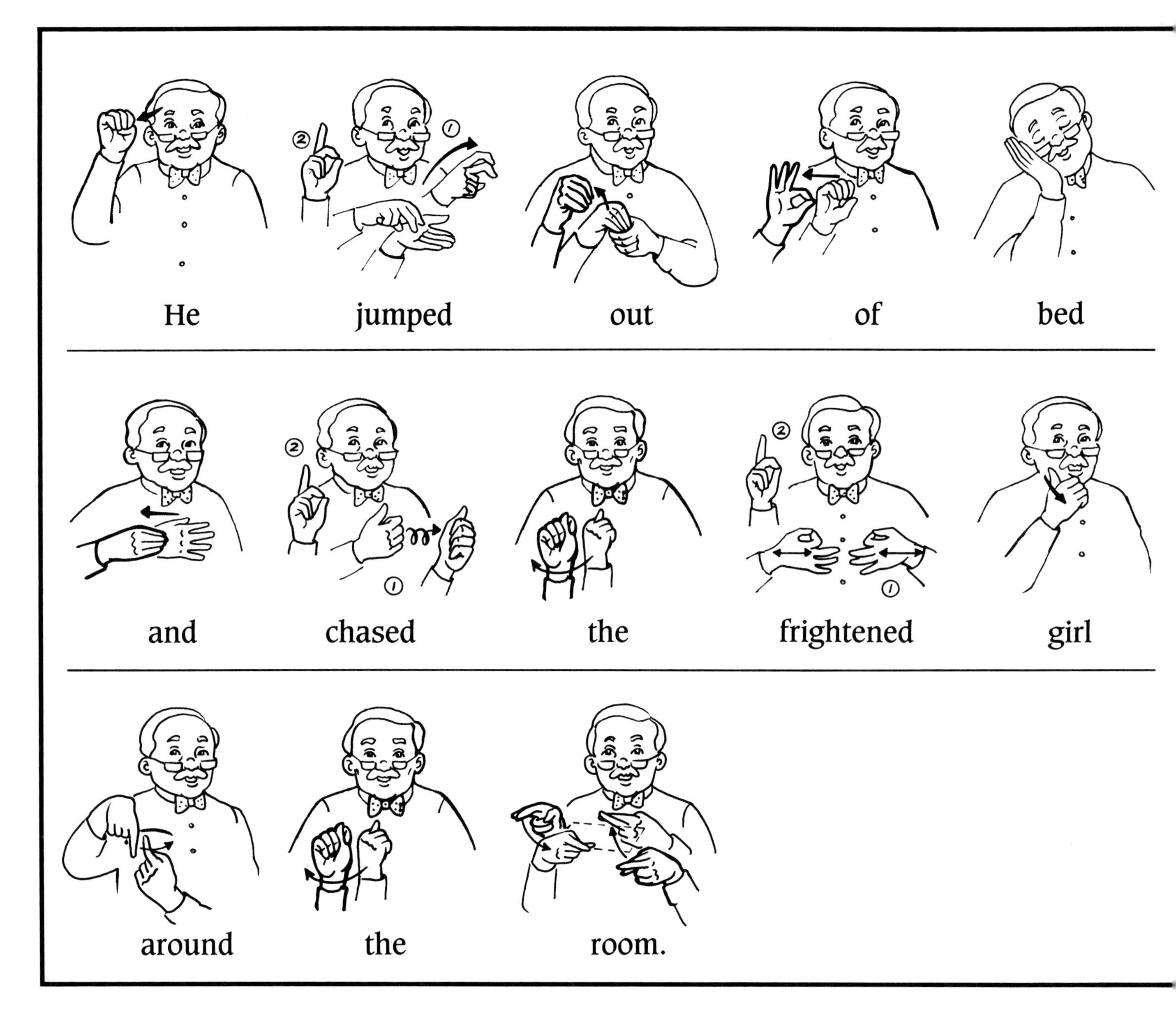
He
jumped
out
of
bed
and
chased
the
frightened
girl
around
the
room.

He jumped out of bed
and chased the frightened girl
around the room.

"Help! Help!" she screamed. "Save me!"

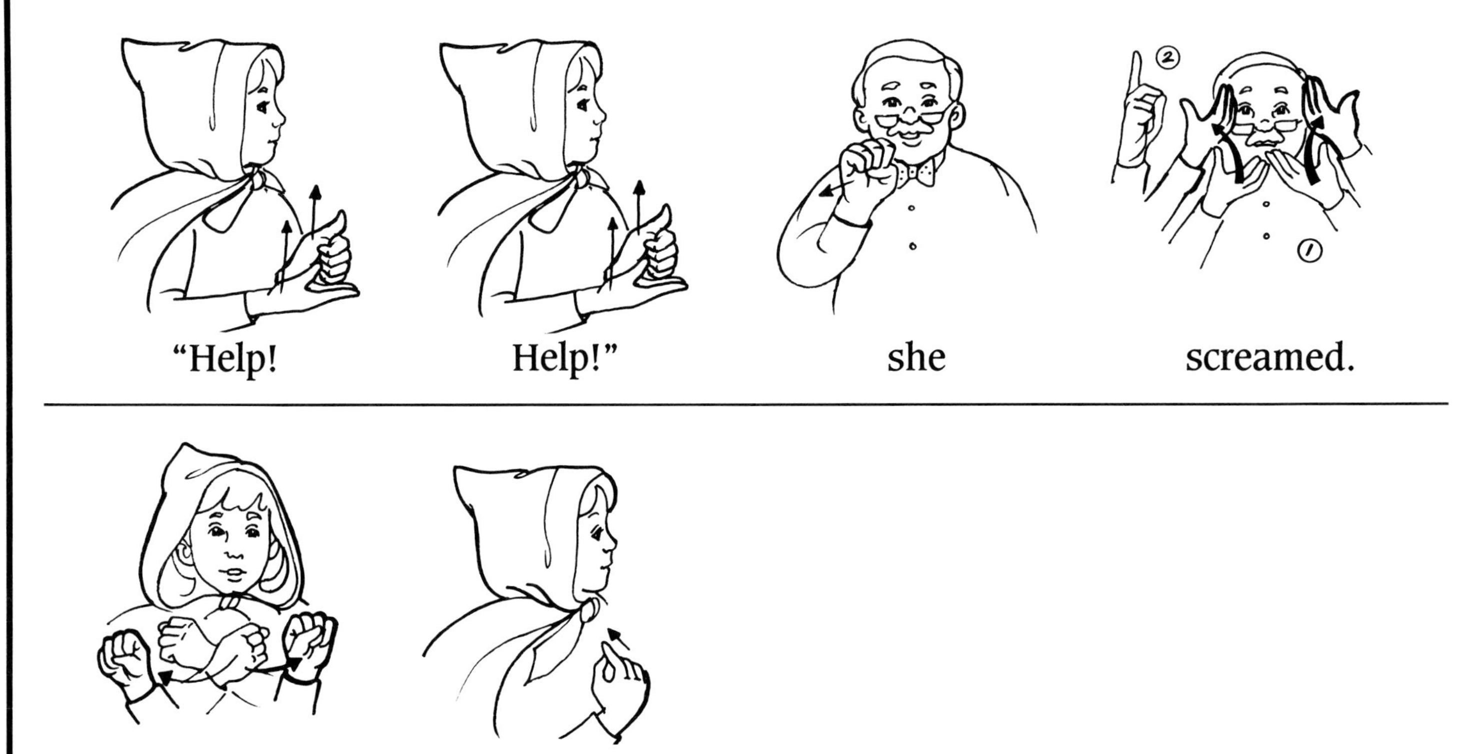
"Help!
Help!"
she
screamed.
"Save
me!"

A hunter heard Little Red Riding Hood scream.
A
hunter
heard
Little
Red
Riding
Hood
scream.

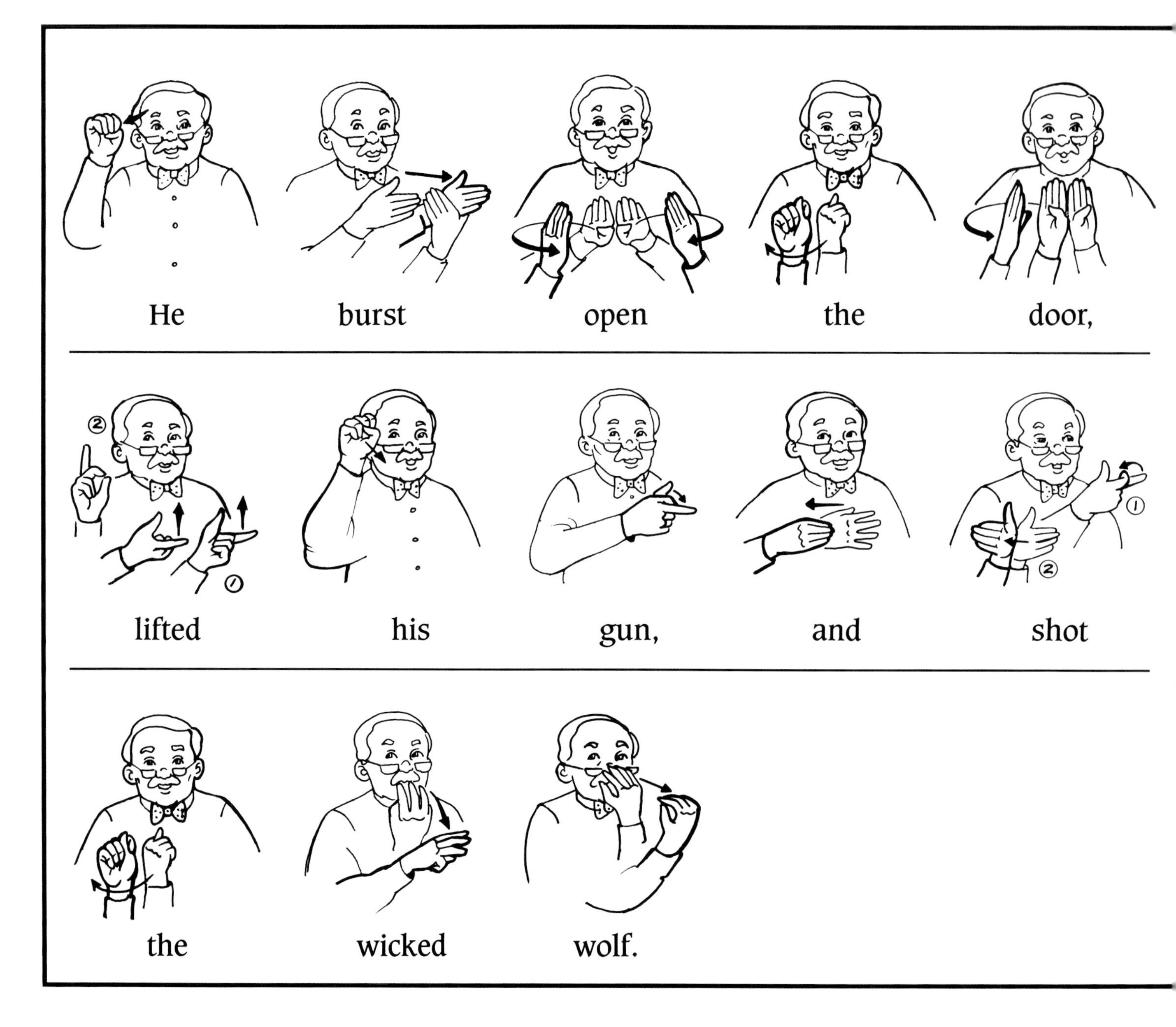
He
burst
open
the
door,
lifted
his
gun,
and
shot
the
wicked
wolf.

He burst open the door, lifted his gun, and shot the wicked wolf.

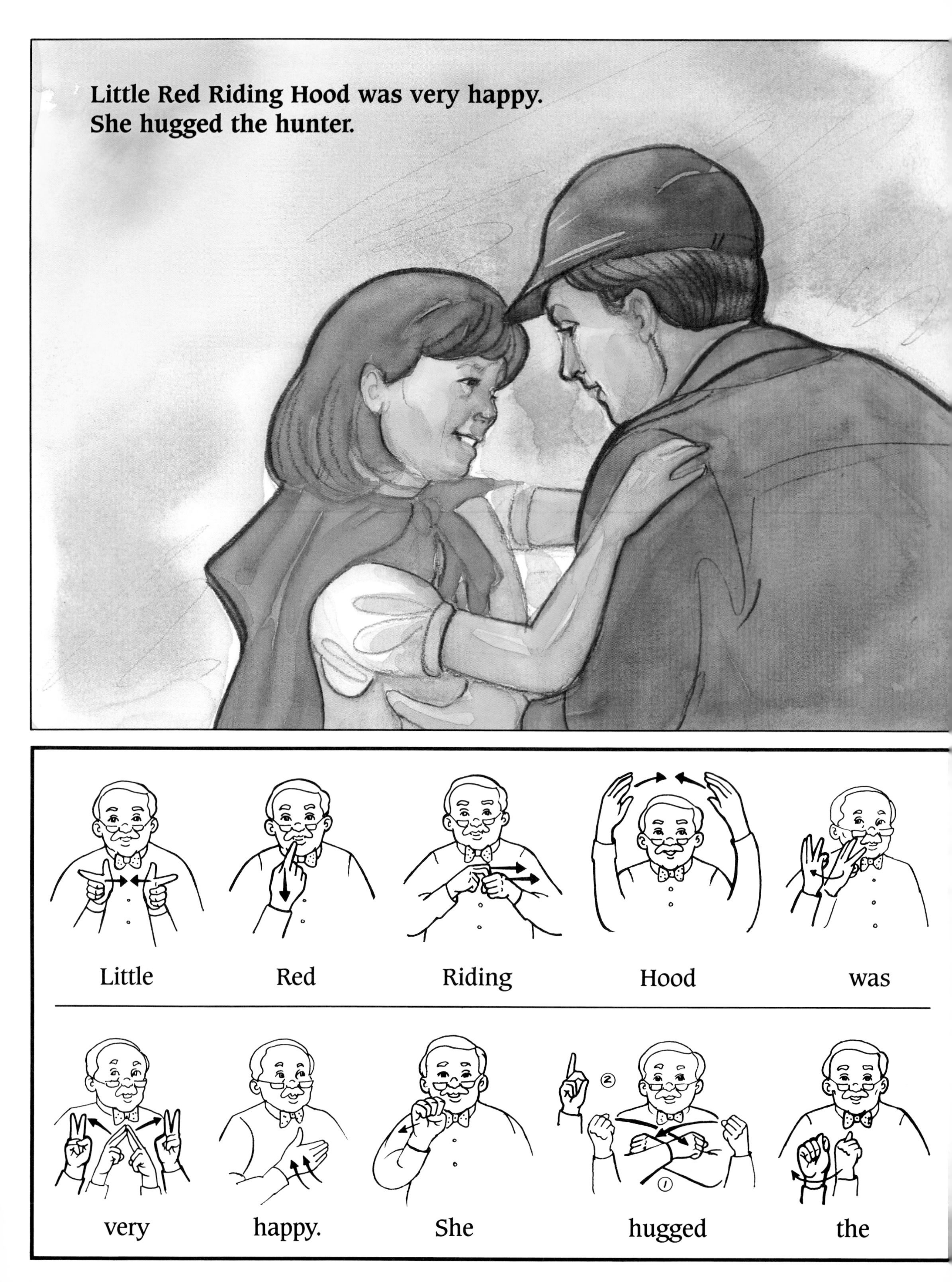
Little Red Riding Hood was very happy.
She hugged the hunter.
Little
Red
Riding
Hood
was
very
happy.
She
hugged
the

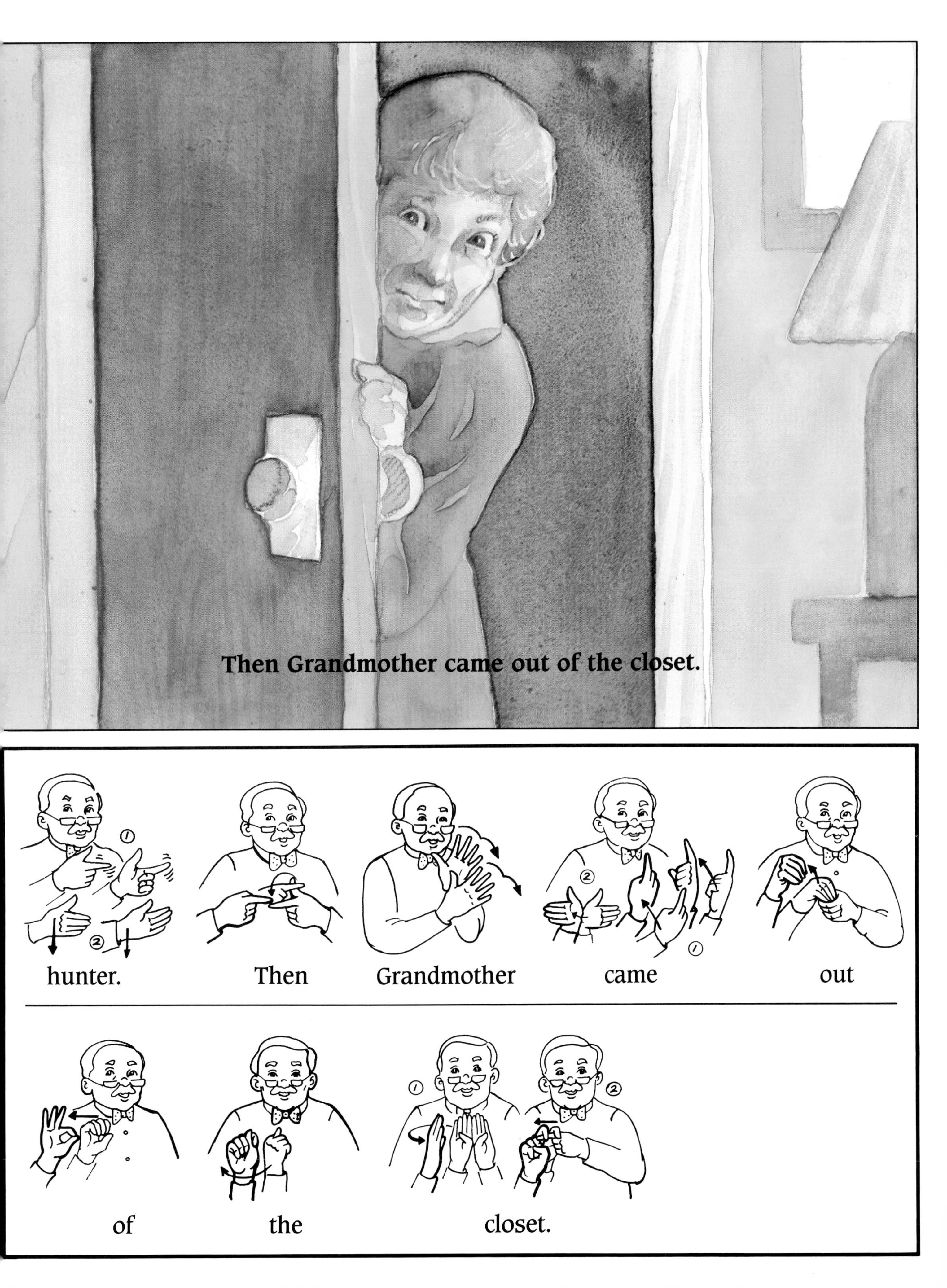
Then Grandmother came out of the closet.
hunter.
Then
Grandmother
came
out
of
the
closet.

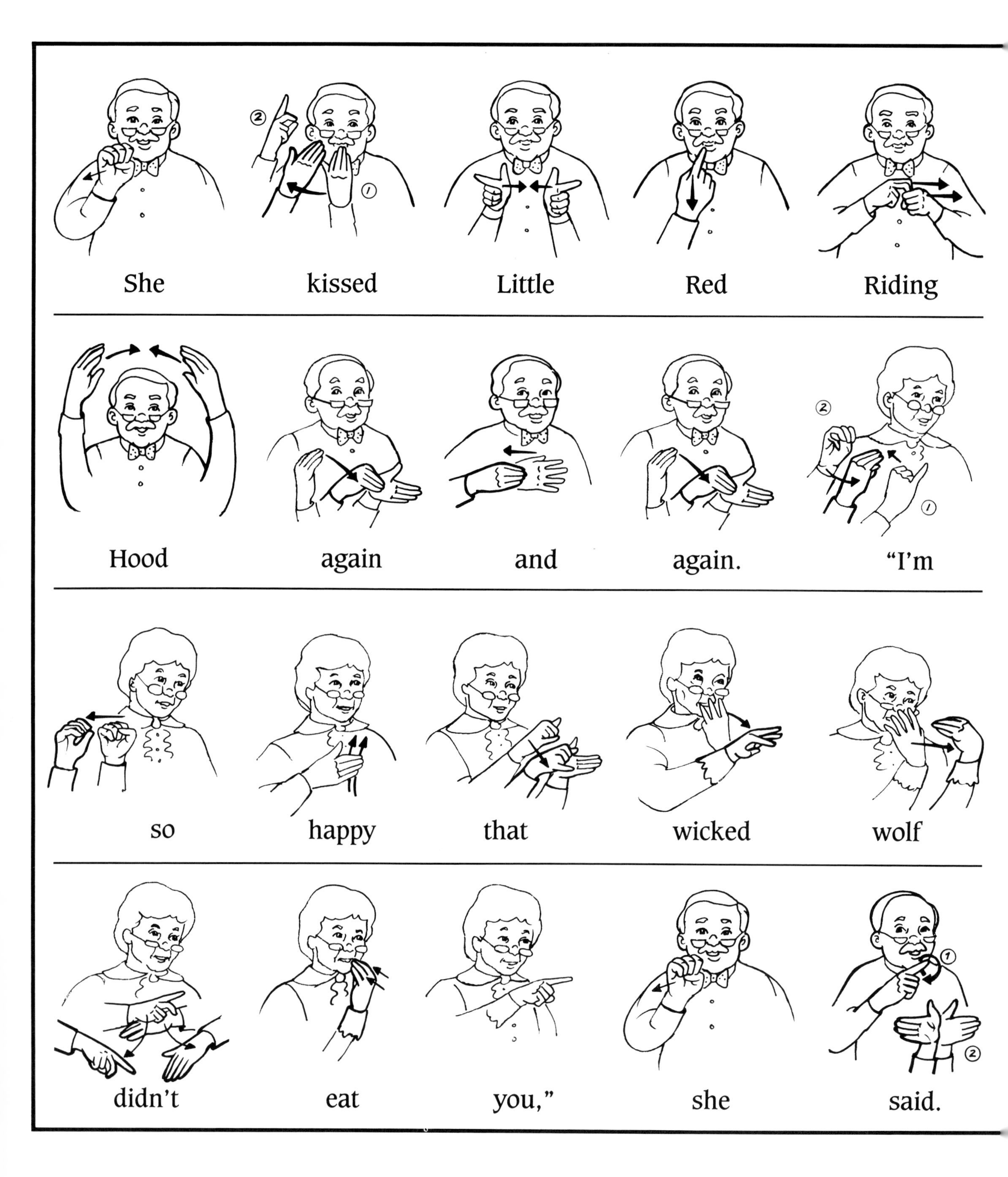
She kissed Little Red Riding
Hood again and again. "I'm
so happy that wicked wolf
didn't eat you," she said.

She kissed Little Red Riding Hood again and again.
"I'm so happy that wicked wolf didn't eat you," she said.

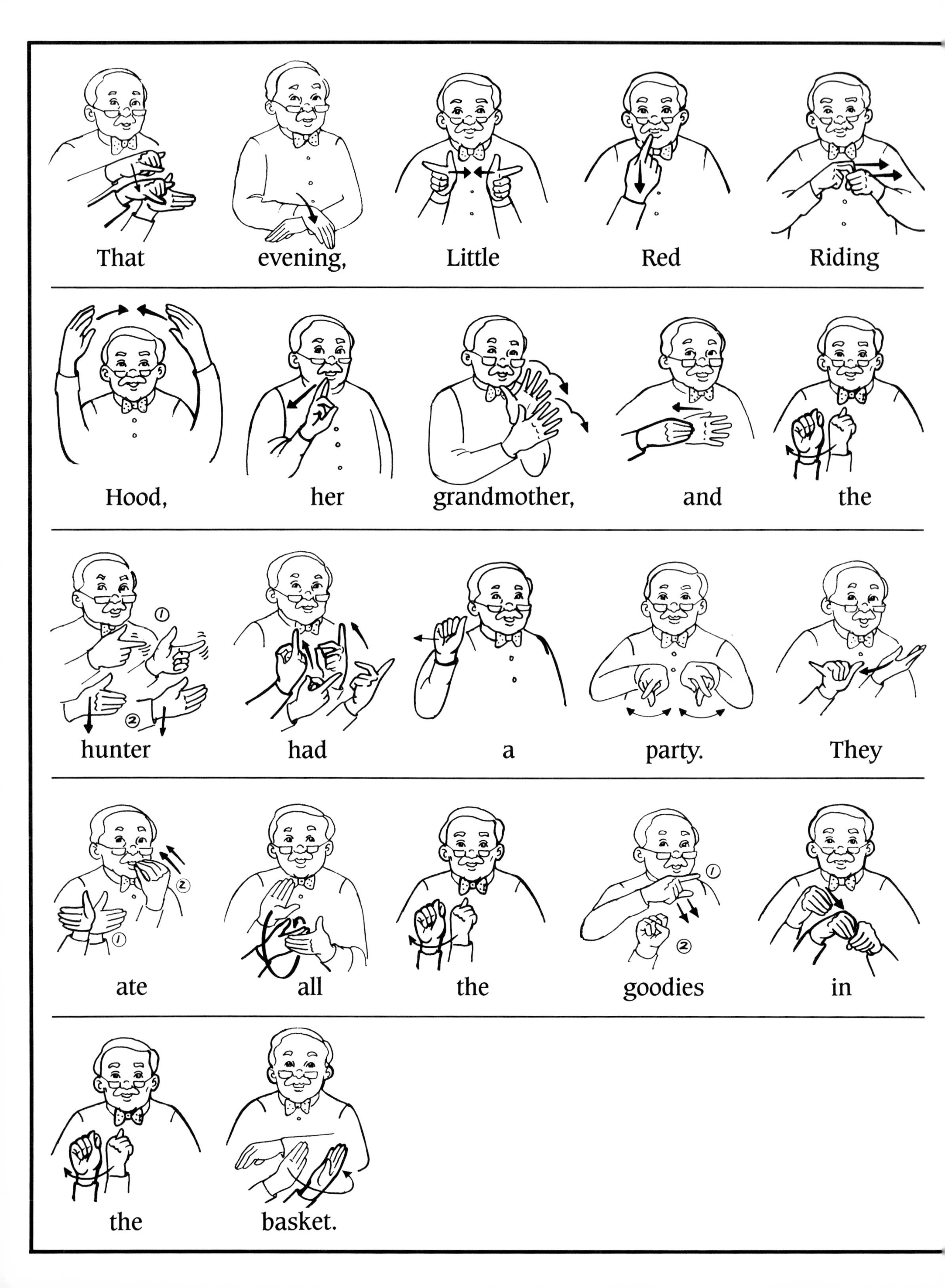

That
evening,
Little
Red
Riding
Hood,
her
grandmother,
and
the
hunter
had
a
party.
They
ate
all
the
goodies
in
the
basket.

That evening, Little Red Riding Hood, her grandmother,
and the hunter had a party. They ate all the goodies in the basket.

Children can learn more about sign language and deafness from the following books:

Buffy's Orange Leash, by Stephen Golder and Lise Memling, illustrated by Marcy Ramsey. Buffy, a Hearing Dog, helps the Johnson family by alerting them to sounds like the telephone and doorbell, and even when their young son Billy is crying.

ISBN 0-930323-42-4, 8½" x 7" hardcover, 32 pages, full-color illustrations

Chris Gets Ear Tubes, by Betty Pace, illustrated by Kathryn Hutton. Chris just couldn't hear right, and always he shouted "What?" when anyone spoke. This book tells what happens before, during, and after surgery for ear tubes in easy-to-understand language that will take away children's fear.

ISBN 0-930323-36-X, 7" x 9" softcover, 48 pages, full-color illustrations

I Can Sign My ABCs, by Susan Chaplin, illustrated by Laura McCaul. This full-color book has 26 signs, each with its manual alphabet handshape followed by the picture, the name, and the sign for a simple object beginning with that letter, an ideal book for teaching both the English and the American Manual alphabets.

ISBN 0-930323-19-X, 7" x 7½" hardcover, 56 pages, full-color illustrations

King Midas *With Selected Sentences in American Sign Language,* adapted by Robert Newby, illustrated by Dawn Majewski and Sandy Cozzolino. This classic, fully illustrated, tale of King Midas, who turns everything he touches into gold, is told accompanied by line drawings of 44 selected sentences in American Sign Language, and 120 signs for different vocabulary words.

ISBN 0-930323-75-0, 8½" x 11" hardcover, 64 pages, full-color illustrations, line drawings

King Midas Videotape, the companion to the book, features renowned deaf actor Mike Lamitola first explaining in sign language ten key sentences and signs for important vocabulary words. Then, while dressed in full costume, he signs and performs the complete story, showing the full elegance and beauty of American Sign Language.

ISBN 0-930323-71-8, VHS, 30 minutes
ISBN 0-930323-77-7, book and videotape

My First Book of Sign, Pamela J. Baker, illustrated by Patricia Bellan Gillen. This alphabet book gives the signs for the 150 words most frequently used by young children. The text includes complete explanations on how to form each sign.

ISBN 0-930323-20-3, 9" x 12" hardcover, full-color illustrations

My Signing Book of Numbers, by Patricia Bellan Gillen. Children can learn their numbers in sign language from this book, which has the appropriate number of things or creatures for numbers 0 through 20, 30, 40, 50, 60, 70, 80, 90, 100, and 1,000.

ISBN 0-930323-37-8, 9" x 12" hardcover, 56 pages, full-color illustrations

Now I Understand, by Gregory S. LaMore, illustrated by Jan Ensing-Keelan. At first, the new boy's schoolmates don't understand why he never answers their questions, and they become angry. Then, their teacher explains that he is hard of hearing, which helps the children to understand about hearing loss and "mainstreaming."

ISBN 0-930323-13-0, 5½" x 8½" flexicover, 52 pages, full-color illustrations

A Very Special Friend, by Dorothy Hoffman Levi, illustrated by Ethel Gold. Frannie, who is six, finds a very special friend. She meets Laura, who "talks" in sign language. Laura teaches Frannie signing, and they become fast friends.

ISBN 0-930323-55-6, 8½" x 7" hardcover, 32 pages, full-color illustrations

You can order these books at your local bookstore or by calling toll-free 1-800-451-1073.